U0512402

文
景

Horizon

社 科 新 知　文 艺 新 潮

沉默的经典

合作农场的冬日食谱

中英双语版

Winter Recipes from the Collective

［美］露易丝·格丽克 著 范静哗 译

上海人民出版社

献给凯瑟琳·戴维斯

For Kathryn Davis

目　录

POEM

Day and night come

hand in hand like a boy and a girl

pausing only to eat wild berries out of a dish

painted with pictures of birds.

They climb the high ice-covered mountain,

then they fly away. But you and I

don't do such things —

We climb the same mountain;

I say a prayer for the wind to lift us

but it does no good;

you hide your head so as not

to see the end —

诗

日夜轮转，

挽手而来，就像一对男孩女孩

停下，只为吃盘中的野浆果，

那盘子绘着几只鸟。

他们攀爬冰雪覆盖的高山，

然后飞走。但你我

不做这样的事 ——

我们攀爬同一座山；

我念一句祷文，愿风将我们托起，

可它没有应验；

你埋下头，以免

看到结局 ——

Downward and downward and downward and downward

is where the wind is taking us;

I try to comfort you

but words are not the answer;

I sing to you as mother sang to me —

Your eyes are closed. We pass

the boy and girl we saw at the beginning;

now they are standing on a wooden bridge;

I can see their house behind them;

How fast you go they call to us,

but no, the wind is in our ears,

that is what we hear —

And then we are simply falling —

And the world goes by,

向下向下再向下还向下，

风就这么携着我们下去；

我有心安慰你，

但言语成不了答案；

我给你唱歌，就像妈妈唱给我听 ——

你闭着眼睛。我们经过

开始时看到的那对男孩女孩；

现在他们站在一座木桥上；

我可以看到他们身后的家；

你们走太快啦，他们对我们喊，

然而，没用，我们的耳朵灌满了风，

那才是我们听到的 ——

然后我们只是坠落 ——

世界流去，

all the worlds, each more beautiful than the last;

I touch your cheek to protect you —

所有的世界，每个都比前一个更美；

我抚摸你的脸，以此保护你 ——

THE DENIAL OF DEATH

1. A TRAVEL DIARY

I had left my passport at an inn we stayed at for a night or so

whose name I couldn't remember. This is how it began.

The next hotel would not receive me,

a beautiful hotel, in an orange grove, with a view of the sea.

How casually you accepted

the room that would have been ours,

and, later, how merrily you stood on the balcony,

pelting me with foil-wrapped chocolates. The next day

you resumed the journey we would have taken together.

The concierge procured an old blanket for me.

By day, I sat outside the kitchen. By night, I spread my blanket

among the orange trees. Every day the same, except for the weather.

拒斥死亡

1. 旅行日记

我们在一家小旅店差不多住了一夜，我把护照落下了，
店名我不记得。这就是整件事的开始。
下一家宾馆不让我入住，
很漂亮的宾馆，在一座柑橘园中，有海景。
你那么轻巧就顶下了
原本属于我们的房间，
接着，你那么欢欣地站在阳台上，
向我不停抛投锡纸包好的巧克力。第二天，
我们本应同行的旅程，由你继续。

礼宾部给我弄来一条旧毯子。
白天，我坐在厨房外。晚上，我把毯子
铺在柑橘树间。每天如此，除非天气有变。

After a time, the staff took pity on me.

The busboy would bring me food from the evening meal,

the odd potato or bit of lamb. Sometimes a postcard arrived.

On the front, glossy landmarks and works of art.

Once, a mountain covered in snow. After a month or so,

there was a postscript: *X sends regards.*

I say a month, but really I had no idea of time.

The busboy disappeared. There was a new busboy, then one

     more, I believe.

From time to time, one would join me on my blanket.

I loved those days! each one exactly like its predecessor.

There were the stone steps we climbed together

and the little town where we breakfasted. Very far away,

I could see the cove where we used to swim, but not hear anymore

the children calling out to one another, nor hear

you anymore, asking me if I would like a cold drink,

which I always would.

一段时间后，工作人员可怜我了。

服务生会从晚餐饭食中拿吃的送我，

卖相不好的土豆或碎羊肉。我不时收到明信片。

正面，光亮的地标和艺术作品。

有一次，是一座雪山。大概一个月后，

寄来附言：某某问好。

说是一个月，但我对时间真的没感觉。

那名服务生不见了。新来了一个，我觉得后来又来了一个。

时不时地，会有人和我一起坐在毯子上。

那些日子让我喜欢！每一天都和前一天毫无不同。

那儿有我们一起爬过的石阶，

还有我们吃早餐的小镇。远远地，

我能看到我们游过泳的海湾，但再也听不到

孩子们互相呼叫，再也听不见

你询问我要不要来杯冷饮——

我总会要的。

When the postcards stopped, I read the old ones again.

I saw myself standing under the balcony in that rain

of foil-covered kisses, unable to believe you would abandon me,

begging you, of course, though not in words —

The concierge, I realized, had been standing beside me.

Do not be sad, he said. You have begun your own journey,

not into the world, like your friend's, but into yourself and your

     memories.

As they fall away, perhaps you will attain

that enviable emptiness into which

all things flow, like the empty cup in the Daodejing —

Everything is change, he said, and everything is connected.

Also everything returns, but what returns is not

what went away —

We watched you walk away. Down the stone steps

and into the little town. I felt

something true had been spoken

当明信片不再寄来时，我重看以前的那些。

我看见自己站在阳台下，锡纸包起的巧克力

如雨而下，无法相信你会弃我而去，

当然，我求你，不过不是用言语——

我意识到礼宾员一直站在我身边。

别难过，他说。你已开始了自己的旅程，

不像你朋友那样走进这个世界，而是走进你自己和你的

　　记忆。

当它们逐渐消失，也许你会获得

那种令人羡慕的空虚，

万物流入其中，犹如《道德经》中的空器皿[1]——

他说，一切都是变，一切都相互关联。

而且，一切都会返回，但返回的

已非当时离开的——

我们看着你走开。走下石阶，

走进小镇。我感觉

某种真实的东西被人说了出来，

and though I would have preferred to have spoken it myself

I was glad at least to have heard it.

2. THE STORY OF THE PASSPORT

It came back but you did not come back.

It happened as follows:

One day an envelope arrived,

bearing stamps from a small European republic.

This the concierge handed me with an air of great ceremony;

I tried to open it in the same spirit.

Inside was my passport.

There was my face, or what had been my face

at some point, deep in the past.

But I had parted ways with it,

that face smiling with such conviction,

filled with all the memories of our travels together

and our dreams of other journeys —

虽然我更希望是我自己说出来的，

但起码我有幸亲耳听到。

2. 护照的故事

护照回来了，但你没回来。

事情是这样的：

有一天，有人寄来一封信，

信封上有某个欧洲小国的邮票。

礼宾员仪式感十足地将它递交给我；

我试图本着同样的精神打开它。

里面是我的护照。

那儿有我的脸，或者我某个时刻

曾有的脸，深陷于过去。

但我已和它分道扬镳，

那张微笑的脸，带着坚定的信念，

弥漫着我们所有旅程的全部回忆

以及我们的其他旅行梦想 ——

I threw it into the sea.

It sank immediately.

Downward, downward, while I continued

staring into the empty water.

All this time the concierge was watching me.

Come, he said, taking my arm. And we began

to walk around the lake, as was my daily habit.

I see, he said, that you no longer

wish to resume your former life,

to move, that is, in a straight line as time

suggests we do, but rather (here he gestured toward the lake)

in a circle which aspires to

that stillness at the heart of things,

though I prefer to think it also resembles a clock.

Here he took out of his pocket

我把它扔进海里。

它立即沉没。
向下，向下，而我继续
凝视着空荡荡的水面。

礼宾员一直看着我。
来吧，他说，挎着我胳膊。我们开始
绕湖散步，这已成为我的日常习惯。

我明白了，他说，你再不想
重拾以前的生活，
就是说，不想活成一条直线，按时间
指引我们的方式，而是要（这时他指着湖面）
活成一个圆环，追求
万事核心的那种静止，
虽然我更愿意把它想成一面时钟。

说到这儿，他从口袋里掏出

the large watch that was always with him. I challenge you, he said,

to tell, looking at this, if it is Monday or Tuesday.

But if you look at the hand that holds it, you will realize I am not

a young man anymore, my hair is silver.

Nor will you be surprised to learn

it was once dark, as yours must have been dark,

and curly, I would say.

Through this recital, we were both

watching a group of children playing in the shallows,

each body circled by a rubber tube.

Red and blue, green and yellow,

a rainbow of children splashing in the clear lake.

I could hear the clock ticking,

presumably alluding to the passage of time

while in fact annulling it.

You must ask yourself, he said, if you deceive yourself.

By which I mean looking at the watch and not

the hand holding it. We stood awhile, staring at the lake,

总是随身携带的大怀表。他说，我赌你看着这块表

也说不出今天星期一还是星期二。

但你若看看握着它的手，就会意识到

我不再年轻，已经头发银白。

你也不会惊讶于它曾经

浓黑，而我敢说，你的头发肯定也曾

又黑，又卷。

这场絮叨之后，我们都看着

一群孩子在浅滩玩耍，

每个身体都套着橡胶游泳圈。

红与蓝，绿与黄，

孩子们在清澈的湖水中嬉戏成一道彩虹。

我听得见滴答的钟声，

按说那是体现时间的流逝，

实际上却是消解时间。

你必须问问自己，他说，你是否在欺骗自己。

我的意思是，看手表而不看

拿着表的手。我们站了一会儿，凝视着湖面，

each of us thinking our own thoughts.

But isn't the life of the philosopher
exactly as you describe, I said. Going over the same course,
waiting for truth to disclose itself.

But you have stopped making things, he said, which is what
the philosopher does. Remember when you kept what you called
your travel journal? You used to read it to me,
I remember it was filled with stories of every kind,
mostly love stories and stories about loss, punctuated
with fantastic details such as wouldn't occur to most of us,

and yet hearing them I had a sense I was listening
to my own experience but more beautifully related
than I could ever have done. I felt
you were talking to me or about me though I never left your side.
What was it called? A travel diary, I think you said,
though I often called it *The Denial of Death*, after Ernest Becker.
And you had an odd name for me, I remember.

每个人都在想自己的心事。

我说，但这不正是哲人的生活，
正如你所描述的那样吗？走同样的路，
等待真相自行揭晓。

但你已停止臆造，他说，那是
哲人所为。记得当年吗，那时你坚持写
你所谓的旅行日志？你曾经读给我听，
我记得里面有各种各样的故事，
大多故事有关爱情和丧失，穿插着
我们大多数人不会想到的奇妙细节，

然而我听的时候，有一种
感觉，像在听我自己的经验，那样的诉说
比我能说出的更加美好。我感觉
你要么是对我说话要么是谈论我，尽管我从未离开你身边。
那叫什么来着？叫旅行日记，你似乎说过，
不过我经常称它为《拒斥死亡》，套用欧内斯特·贝克尔的
　　书名。[2]

Concierge, I said. *Concierge* is what I called you.

And before that, *you*, which is, I believe,

a convention in fiction.

我记得，你给我取了一个奇怪的名字。

礼宾员，我说。礼宾员是我对你的称呼。

在那之前，将你称为你，我相信

这是虚构作品的一个惯例。

WINTER RECIPES FROM THE COLLECTIVE

1.

Each year when winter came, the old men entered

the woods to gather the moss that grew

on the north side of certain junipers.

It was slow work, taking many days, though these

were short days because the light was waning,

and when their packs were full, painfully

they made their way home, moss being heavy to carry.

The wives fermented these mosses, a time-consuming project

especially for people so old

they had been born in another century.

But they had patience, these elderly men and women,

such as you and I can hardly imagine,

and when the moss was cured, it was with wild mustards and

合作农场的冬日食谱

1

每当冬天来临，老人们就会进入
树林，采集只长在
特定刺柏树阴面的苔藓。
这是慢工细活，需要好多天，尽管
光线减弱，白天变得很短，
当他们装满背包，回家的路
就走得很吃力，苔藓重得背不动。
女人们给这些苔藓发酵，一项耗时的工程，
尤其对这些老人来说，
她们都生于另一个世纪。
但他们有的是耐心，这些老头老太，
你我这样的人难以想象的那种耐心，
苔藓发酵完以后，拌进野芥菜和硬梗草

sturdy herbs

packed between the halves of ciabattine, and weighted like pan

    bagnat,

after which the thing was done: an "invigorating winter sandwich"

it was called, but no one said

it was good to eat; it was what you ate

when there was nothing else, like matzoh in the desert, which

our parents called the bread of affliction— Some years

an old man would not return from the woods, and then his wife

    would need

a new life, as a nurse's helper, or to supervise

the young people who did the heavy work, or to sell

the sandwiches in the open market as the snow fell, wrapped

in wax paper— The book contains

only recipes for winter, when life is hard. In spring,

anyone can make a fine meal.

2.

Of the moss, the prettiest was saved

夹到剖开的拖鞋面包中，像法式三明治那样重，

然后就做成了"冬日回春三明治"，

它叫这个名字，但没人说

它好吃；那是没别的可吃时

人们吃的东西，就像沙漠中的无酵饼，我们父母

称为苦难饼 —— 有几年，

有个老头在树林里不愿回来，而他妻子就需要

过一种新生活，做护理员助手，或者指导

那些做重活的年轻人，或在下雪时

去露天市场兜售裹在蜡纸里的

三明治 —— 本书只收录

冬日食谱，这季节生活艰难。春天时，

谁都能做一顿美餐。

2

最漂亮的苔藓会被留着，

用于盆栽，放在

一个专门的小房间，

不过我们没什么人有这方面的天分，

for bonsai, for which

a small room had been designated,

though few of us had the gift,

and even then a long apprenticeship

was necessary, the rules being complicated.

A bright light shone on the specimen being pruned,

never into animal shapes, which were frowned on,

only into those shapes

natural to the species— Those of us who watched

sometimes chose the container, in my case

a porcelain bowl, given me by my grandmother.

The wind grew harsher around us.

Under the bright light, my friend

who was shaping the tree set down her shears.

The tree seemed beautiful to me,

not finished perhaps, still it was beautiful, the moss

draped around its roots— I was not

permitted to prune it but I held the bowl in my hands,

a pine blowing in high wind

like man in the universe.

即便有，也得经过

漫长的学徒期，而规则又很繁杂。

一道亮光照在正被修剪的样品上，

从没修成动物形状，那让人皱眉头，

只修成植物

自然具有的形状 —— 我们这些参观的人

有时会挑选容器，而我所选的

是一只瓷盆，我祖母送给我的。

四周的风越刮越紧。

在那道亮光下，我那位朋友

放下修树的剪刀。

在我看来，树挺漂亮，

也许还没修剪完成，但已很漂亮，

它的根须披着苔藓 —— 我不可以

动剪刀修，但我手捧着盆子，

一棵松树在疾风中摇动，

就像人在宇宙中。

3.

As I said, the work was hard—

not simply caring for the little trees

but caring for ourselves as well,

feeding ourselves, cleaning the public rooms—

But the trees were everything.

And how sad we were when one died,

and they do die, despite having been

removed from nature; all things die eventually.

I minded most with the ones that lost their leaves,

which would pile up on the moss and stones—

The trees were miniature, as I have said,

but there is no such thing as death in miniature.

Shadows passing over the snow,

steps approaching and going away.

The dead leaves lay on the stones;

there was no wind to lift them.

3

如我所说，活儿很辛苦 ——

不仅要照顾小树，

还要照顾我们自己，

吃饭，打扫公用房间 ——

但树是一切。

死一棵树，我们都那么悲伤，

而它们的确会死，尽管

已经被移出自然环境；万物终有一死。

我最在意的是那些脱了叶的树，

叶子堆积在苔藓和石头上 ——

如我所说，这些树是迷你的，

但没有迷你死亡之说。

影子掠过白雪，

脚步走近又离开。

死叶留在石上；

没有风吹起它们。

4.

It was as dark as it would ever be

but then I knew to expect this,

the month being December, the month of darkness.

It was early morning. I was walking

from my room to the arboretum; for obvious reasons,

we were encouraged never to be alone,

but exceptions were made— I could see

the arboretum glowing across the snow;

the trees had been hung with tiny lights,

I remember thinking how they must be

visible from far away, not that we went, mainly,

far away— Everything was still.

In the kitchen, sandwiches were being wrapped for market.

My friend used to do this work.

Huli songli, our instructor called her,

giver of care. I remember

watching her: inside the door,

procedures written on a card in Chinese characters

4

黑暗如常，也一贯如此，

于是我明白这在预料之中，

十二月了，黑暗的月份。

正是清晨。我从房间

走到植物园；出于显然的原因，

我们得到的叮嘱是千万不要单独行动，

但也有例外 —— 我看得到

植物园在雪地的另一边闪亮；

树上挂满小灯，

我记得当时我想它们肯定从很远处

就能看到，倒不是我们多数时候

会走那么远 —— 一切都没动。

厨房里有人在打包三明治，准备送到集市。

以前是我朋友操持这事。

我们的指导员称呼她"送礼护理"[3]，

意为"爱心赠送员"。我记得

我看着她：门背后，

卡片上是用汉字书写的步骤，

translated as *the same things in the same order,*

and underneath: *We have deprived them of their origins,*

they have come to need us now.

译文是相同的东西排成相同的顺序，

而那下面是：它们的根已被我们剥夺，

现在它们需要的是我们。

WINTER JOURNEY

Well, it was just as I thought,

the path

all but obliterated—

We had moved then

from the first to the second stage,

from the dream to the proposition.

And look—

here is the line between,

resembling

this line from which our words emerge;

moonlight breaks through.

Shadows on the snow

冬之旅

是的，和我想的一样，
小径
几乎湮灭 ——

我们那时已经
从第一阶段过渡到第二阶段，
从梦想过渡到了提议。
看 ——

这里有一条居间的线，
很像
我们语言从中浮现的这条线：
月光喷涌而出。

雪地承接着

cast by pine trees.

*

Say goodbye to standing up,

my sister said. We were sitting on our favorite bench

outside the common room, having

a glass of gin without ice.

Looked a lot like water, so the nurses

smiled at you as they passed,

pleased with how hydrated you were becoming.

Inside the common room, the advanced cases

were watching television under a sign that said

Welcome to Happy Hour.

If you can't read, my sister said,

can you be happy?

We were having a fine old time getting old,

everything hunky-dory as the nurses said,

松树投下的影子。

从此不再站起来，
妹妹宣布。当时我们正在公共休息室外
坐着我们最喜欢的长椅，品着
一杯不加冰的杜松子酒。
那看起来很像水，所以护士
经过时都对你微笑，
为你一直补水而高兴。

公共休息室内，晚期病患
在看电视，电视机上方的标语写着
欢迎加入开心时光。
我妹妹说，如果你不识字，
你能快乐吗？

我们逐渐变老，将时光过成美好的往昔，
可称万事遂意，正如护士所言，

though you could tell

snow was beginning to fall,

not fall exactly, more like weave side to side,

sliding around in the sky—

*

Now we are home, my mother said;

before, we were at Aunt Posy's.

And, between, in the car, the Pontiac,

driving from Hewlett to Woodmere.

You children, my mother said, must sleep

as much as possible. Lights

were shining in the trees:

those are the stars, my mother said.

Then I was in my bed. How could the stars be there

when there were no trees?

On the ceiling, silly, that's where they were.

虽然你看得出来

天已开始落雪，

也不能说是落，更像是飘飘洒洒，

在天空中绕圈滑动 ——

＊

现在我们到家了，妈妈说；

之前，我们在波西阿姨家。

在那时和现在之间，在那辆庞蒂亚克车里，

车从休利特开到伍德米尔。[4]

你们几个孩子，我妈说，必须睡觉，

越多越好。树上，

灯闪闪发光：

那些是星星，妈妈说。

然后我就在床上了。那儿没有树，

怎么会有星星呢?

在天花板上，傻孩子，那是它们的地盘。

*

I must say

I was very tired walking along the road,

very tired— I put my hat on a snowbank.

Even then I was not light enough,

my body a burden to me.

Along the path, there were

things that had died along the way—

lumps of snow,

that's what they were—

The wind blew. Nights I could see

shadows of the pines, the moon

was that bright.

*

必须承认，

我在这条路上走得很累，

真的累 —— 我把帽子放在雪堤上。

即便如此，我还不够轻巧，

身体成了我的负担。

整条小径上

都有在路边死去的东西 ——

成堆的雪，

它们看起来就是这样 ——

风吹起来的。我夜夜可见

松树的身影，月色

那么明亮。

Every hour or so, my friend turned to wave at me,

or I believed she did, though

the dark obscured her.

Still her presence sustained me:

some of you will know what I mean.

差不多每个钟头，我朋友就会转身向我挥手，

或者我以为她挥了手，尽管

黑暗令她朦胧不清。

不过她的存在支撑着我：

你们会有人明白我的意思。

NIGHT THOUGHTS

Long ago I was born.

There is no one alive anymore

who remembers me as a baby.

Was I a good baby? A

bad? Except in my head

that debate is now

silenced forever.

What constitutes

a bad baby, I wondered. Colic,

my mother said, which meant

it cried a lot.

What harm could there be

in that? How hard it was

to be alive, no wonder

they all died. And how small

静夜思

很久以前，我出生了。
已没有在世的人
还记得我小时候。
我是个乖宝宝吗？
我不乖？这争论
已永远被消音，
除了在我脑海里。
什么会导致
宝宝不乖，我不懂。妈妈说，
腹部绞痛，这意味着
宝宝会哭得很凶。
那会有什么
危害？要活着
可真难啊，难怪
他们都死了。那时我该是

I must have been, suspended

in my mother, being patted by her

approvingly.

What a shame I became

verbal, with no connection

to that memory. My mother's love!

All too soon I emerged

my true self,

robust but sour,

like an alarm clock.

多么小啊，悬吊

在妈妈怀里，接受着

她赞许的轻拍。

多让人遗憾，我开始

学会说话，却与那记忆

断了关联。我妈妈的爱！

很快，我就显露了

真实的自我，

强壮但刻薄，

像一只闹钟。

AN ENDLESS STORY

1.

Halfway through the sentence

she fell asleep. She had been telling

some sort of fable concerning

a young girl who wakens one morning

as a bird. So like life,

said the person next to me. I wonder,

he went on, do you suppose our friend here

plans to fly away when she wakens?

The room was very quiet.

We were both studying her; in fact,

everyone in the room was studying her.

To me, she seemed as before, though

her head was slumped on her chest; still,

讲不完的故事

1

一句话讲到一半，
她睡着了。她一直在讲
一个寓言式故事，
关于一个女孩早上醒来
变成了一只鸟。人生也如此，
我身边的人说。他继续道，
我想知道你怎么想，我们这个朋友
醒来时打算飞走吗？
房间很安静。
我们都在审视她；实际上，
房间里的每个人都在审视她。
对我来说，她似乎一如从前，虽然
她的头垂在胸前；不过，

her color was good— She seems to be breathing,

my neighbor said. Not only that, he went on,

we are all of us in this room breathing—

just how you want a story to end. And yet,

he added, we may never know

whether the story was intended to be

a cautionary tale or perhaps a love story,

since it has been interrupted. So we cannot be certain

we have as yet experienced the end.

But who does, he said. Who does?

2.

We stayed like this a long time,

stranded, I thought to myself,

like ships paralyzed by bad weather.

My neighbor had withdrawn into himself.

Something, I felt, existed between us,

nothing so final as a baby,

but real nevertheless—

气色很好 —— 我邻座说，

似乎还在呼吸。他继续说，

我们，这房间里所有的人都在呼吸 ——

这是你希望一个故事结束的方式。然而，

他补充道，我们可能永远

不知道这故事意在成为

一部醒世小说还是一个爱情故事，

因为它被打断了。所以我们不能确定

我们是否还没经历那个结局。

但谁经历过呢，他说。谁？

2

我们就像这样待了很久，

搁浅了，我心想，

就像恶劣天气下瘫痪的船。

我邻座已躲进他自己。

我觉得我们之间隔着什么，

绝非婴儿那样具体，

但仍然很真实 ——

Meanwhile, no one spoke.

No one rushed to get help

or knelt beside the prone woman.

The sun was going down; long shadows of the elms

spread like dark lakes over the grass.

Finally my neighbor raised his head.

Clearly, he said, someone must finish this story

which was, I believe, to have been

a love story such as silly women tell, meaning

very long, filled with tangents and distractions

meant to disguise the fundamental

tedium of its simplicities. But as, he said,

we have changed riders, we may as well change

horses at the same time. Now that the tale is mine,

I prefer that it be a meditation on existence.

The room grew very still.

I know what you think, he said; we all despise

stories that seem dry and interminable, but mine

will be a true love story,

if by love we mean the way we loved when we were young,

同时，也没人说什么。

没人急匆匆地去求助，

或者跪在趴倒的女人身边。

太阳正在下落；榆树的长影

铺展在草地上，像黑色的湖泊。

最后，邻座抬起头。

他说，显然，必须有人把故事讲完，

我相信这故事大概

是一个傻女人讲的爱情故事，意味着

冗长累赘、枝节横生、时有离题，

目的就在于掩盖

它简单朴素之下的乏味本质。但他说：

既然我们换了赶车人，那最好

同时把马也换了。既然现在故事由我接手，

我更愿意它成为对存在的冥想。

房间变得很安静。

他说，我知道你是怎么想的；对那些显然

枯燥又永无休止的故事，我们都不以为然，

但我将会讲一个真实的爱情故事，

假设我们所说的爱是指我们年轻时那样的相爱，

as though there were no time at all.

3.

Soon night fell. Automatically

the lights came on.

On the floor, the woman moved.

Someone had covered her with a blanket

which she thrust aside.

Is it morning, she said. She had

propped herself up somehow so she could see

the door. There was a bird, she said.

Someone is supposed to kiss it.

Perhaps it has been kissed already, my neighbor said.

Oh no, she said. Once it is kissed

it becomes a human being. So it cannot fly;

it can only sit and stand and lie down.

And kiss, my neighbor waggishly added.

Not anymore, she said. There was just the one time

to break the spell that had frozen its heart.

似乎根本就没有时间这回事。

3

很快，夜幕降临。灯

都自动地亮了。

地板上，女人动了动。

有人给她盖上毯子，

但她推开了。

是早上了吗，她问。她设法

撑起身，让自己看到

门。她说，有一只鸟。

应该有人亲亲它。

说不定已经有人亲过了，我邻座说。

哦，不会吧，她说。一旦有人亲过，

它就会变成人。那它就不会飞；

只会坐、站、躺。

还有亲吻，我邻座俏皮地加了一句。

不再会亲吻了，她说。要打破咒语，

给心脏解冻，机会只有一次。

That was a bad trade, she said,

the wings for the kiss.

She gazed at us, like a figure on top of a mountain

looking down, though we were the ones looking down,

in actual fact. Obviously my mind is not what it was, she said.

Most of my facts have disappeared, but certain

underlying principles have been in consequence

exposed with surprising clarity.

The Chinese were right, she said, to revere the old.

Look at us, she said. We are all of us in this room

still waiting to be transformed. This is why we search for love.

We search for it all of our lives,

even after we find it.

用翅膀换亲吻，她说，

这笔交易不合算。

她盯着我们，就像站在山顶的人

往下看，虽然事实上我们才是

往下看的人。她说，我的脑子显然不同以往。

我谈的大多事实已经消失，但某些

基本原则倒是因此暴露出来，

清晰得令人吃惊。

她说，中国人敬老，这是对的。

她还说，再看看我们。我们在这房间里的每个人

都还在等着脱胎换骨。所以我们才追求爱。

我们追寻了一生，

哪怕找到后还要追寻。

PRESIDENTS' DAY

Lots of good-natured sunshine everywhere

making the snow glitter—quite

lifelike, I thought, nice

to see that again; my hands

were almost warm. Some

principle is at work, I thought:

commendable, taking an interest

in human life, but to be safe

I threw some snow over my shoulder,

since I had no salt. And sure enough

the clouds came back, and sure enough

the sky grew dark and menacing,

all as before, except

the losses were piling up—

And yet, moments ago

总统日

处处洋溢着和暖的阳光，

照耀得雪光熠熠 —— 相当

栩栩如生，我想，又看到这景象

真好；我双手几乎

暖和了。是某种原理

发挥了作用，我想：

对人的生活发生兴趣，

值得嘉许，但为了确保好运，

我还是往背后撒了点雪，

因为没有盐[5]。果然，

乌云回返，果然，

天空转暗，显露出某种威胁，

正如之前那样，只是

不幸都堆积了起来 ——

可就在片刻之前，

the sun was shining. How joyful my head was,

basking in it, getting to feel it first

while the limbs waited. Like a deserted hive.

Joyful—now there's a word

we haven't used in a while.

还是阳光灿烂。我的脑袋多么欢快，

沉浸其中，它是最先感受到这些的，

四肢还在等。像被遗弃的蜂巢。

欢快 —— 这可是一个

我们有一段时间没用过的字眼。

AUTUMN

The part of life

devoted to contemplation

was at odds with the part

committed to action.

*

Fall was approaching.

But I remember

it was always approaching

once school ended.

*

Life, my sister said,

秋

专用于沉思的

这部分人生，

与致力于行动的

那部分相抵触。

秋天在逼近。

但我记得，

学期一结束，

它就总在逼近。

生活，妹妹说，

is like a torch passed now

from the body to the mind.

Sadly, she went on, the mind is not

there to receive it.

The sun was setting.

Ah, the torch, she said.

It has gone out, I believe.

Our best hope is that it's flickering,

fort/ da, fort/ da, like little Ernst

throwing his toy over the side of his crib

and then pulling it back. It's too bad,

she said, there are no children here.

We could learn from them, as Freud did.

*

We would sometimes sit

on benches outside the dining room.

The smell of leaves burning.

就像一把火炬，现在

已从身体传到心灵。

可悲的是，她继续说，心灵

并没有在那里迎接它。

太阳西沉。

啊，火炬，她说。

我想，它已熄灭。

我们最好的希望是它还在闪烁，

失／得，失／得，像小恩斯特[6]

把玩具扔到小床外

再把它拉回来。她说，

真不好玩，这儿没有小孩。

我们可以向他们学习，弗洛伊德就这么说过。

*

我们有时会坐在

餐厅外的长椅上。

有烧树叶的气味。

Old people and fire, she said.

Not a good thing. They burn their houses down.

*

How heavy my mind is,

filled with the past.

Is there enough room

for the world to penetrate?

It must go somewhere,

it cannot simply sit on the surface—

*

Stars gleaming over the water.

The leaves piled, waiting to be lit.

老人与火，她说。

不是什么好事。他们会把房子烧掉。

*

我心思那么沉重，

装满了往事。

还有足够空间

让世界穿透吗?

它必须去一个地方，

不能仅仅停留在表面 ——

*

星星在水面上闪耀。

树叶堆积，等着被点燃。

*

Insight, my sister said.

Now it is here.

But hard to see in the darkness.

You must find your footing

before you put your weight on it.

*

洞察力，妹妹说。

现在就在这里。

但在黑暗中很难看见。

你必须找到立足点，

才能把你的重量放上去。

SECOND WIND

I think this is my second wind,

my sister said. Very

like the first, but that

ended, I remember. Oh

what a wind that was, so powerful

the leaves fell off the trees.

I don't think so,

I said. Well, they were

on the ground, my sister said. Remember

running around the park in Cedarhurst,

jumping on the piles, destroying them?

You never jumped, my mother said.

You were good girls; you stayed where I put you.

Not in our heads,

my sister said. I put

春风二度

我想这是我的春风二度，

妹妹说。非常

像第一度，但那场风

已经刮完，我记得。哦，

那场风好大，很有劲，

树叶都被刮了下来。

我说，我认为

不是那么回事。妹妹说，嗯，

它们就在地上。你还记得

在锡达赫斯特的公园里乱跑，

跳上一堆堆叶子，踩碎它们吗？

你们从来没跳上去过，妈妈说。

你们都是乖乖女；我把你们放在哪儿你们就待在哪儿。

但我们脑子里不这么想，

妹妹说。我双手

my arms around her. What

a brave sister you are,

I said.

搂着她。你真是个

勇敢的妹妹，

我说。

THE SETTING SUN

1.

I'm glad you like it, he said,

since it may be the last of its kind.

There was nothing to say;

in fact, it did seem the end of something.

It was a solemn moment.

We stood awhile in silence, staring at it together.

Outside the sun was setting,

the sort of pointed symmetry

I have always noticed.

If only I'd known, he said,

the effect of words.

落日

1

很高兴你喜欢，他说，

它可能是这一类中的最后一个。

没什么可说的；

事实上，它似乎的确是什么事物的终点。

那是个庄严时刻。

我们肃立片刻，一起注视它。

外面夕阳西沉，

那种显著的对称，

我一直都注意到了。

他说，要是懂得言辞的效应，

那该多好。

Do you see how this thing has acquired weight and importance
since I spoke?

I could have done this long ago, he said,
and not wasted my time beginning over and over.

2.

My teacher was holding a brush
but then I was holding a brush too—
we were standing together watching the canvas
out of the corners of which
a turbulent darkness surged; in the center
was ostensibly a portrait of a dog.
The dog had a kind of forced quality;
I could see that now. I have
never been much good with living things.
Brightness and darkness I do rather well with.
I was very young. Many things had happened
but nothing had happened

你知道我说话之后，这件事有了

怎样的分量和重要性吗？

我早该这样做，他说，

而不是浪费时间—再从头开始。

2

我老师握着画笔，

后来我也拿起了画笔 ——

我们站在一起，看着画布，

看骚动的黑暗

从四角澎湃涌现；而那中心

显然可见一条狗的画像。

那狗有一种被强加的特性；

我现在才可以看出来。

我向来不善于和活的生物相处。

倒是很善于辨别明暗。

我还很年轻。发生过很多事，

却没什么是一再

repeatedly, which makes a difference.

My teacher, who had spoken not a word, began to turn now

to the other students. Sorry as I felt for myself at that moment,

I felt sorrier for my teacher, who always wore the same clothes,

and had no life, or no apparent life,

only a keen sense of what was alive on canvas.

With my free hand, I touched his shoulder.

Why, sir, I asked, have you no comment on the work before us?

I have been blind for many years, he said,

though when I could see I had a subtle and discerning eye,

of which, I believe, there is ample evidence in my own work.

This is why I give you assignments, he said,

and why I question all of you so scrupulously.

As to my current predicament: when I judge from a student's

despair and anger he has become an artist,

then I speak. Tell me, he added,

what do you think of your own work?

Not enough night, I answered. In the night I can see my own soul.

That is also my vision, he said.

发生的，这就效果有别。

我老师一言不发，开始转身

面向其他学生。我当时虽然为自己难过，

但更为老师难过，他总穿着同样的衣服，

没有人生，或者说没有鲜明的人生，

只对画布上的生机有一种敏锐的感觉。

我用空着的手碰了碰他的肩膀。

先生，我问，对我们面前的作品，您为何不做评论呢？

我已失明多年，他说，

不过我还能看见的时候，我眼神敏锐，明察秋毫，

这一点，我相信在我自己的作品中有充分证据。

他说，我给你分配任务，也是基于这个理由，

也因此才这么严谨地质疑你们所有人；

至于我目前的困境：当一个学生的绝望和愤怒

让我判断出他已然是一位艺术家时，

我才说话。你告诉我，他补充道，

你怎么评价你自己的作品？

天还没那么晚，我答道。我只在深夜才能看到自己的灵魂。

那也是我的观点，他说。

3.

I'm against

symmetry, he said. He was holding in both hands

an unbalanced piece of wood that had been

very large once, like the limb of a tree:

this was before its second life in the water,

after which, though there was less of it

in terms of mass, there was greater

spiritual density. Driftwood,

he said, confirms my view—this is why it seems

inherently dramatic. To make this point,

he tapped the wood. Rather violently, it seemed,

because a piece broke off.

Movement! he cried. That is the lesson! Look at these paintings,

he said, meaning ours. I have been making art

longer than you have been breathing

and yet my canvases have life, they are drowning

in life— Here he grew silent.

I stood beside my work, which now seemed rigid and lifeless.

3

我反对对称性，

他说。他双手捧着

一块不平衡的木头，曾经

非常大，像树的大枝：

那是它在水中获得第二次生命之前，

而之后，虽然就质量而言，

它更小了，但有了更大的

精神密度。他说，浮木

证实了我的观点 —— 这解释了它为何

似乎有了内在戏剧性。他敲了敲木头，

以示强调。但似乎敲得太猛，

木头掉下一块。

运动！他喊道。那是教训所在！看看这些画，

他说，意指我们的作品。我一直从事艺术创作，

比你呼吸的时间还长，

然而我的画布生机勃勃，全都沉浸

在生命中 —— 说到此，他沉默了。

我站在我的作品旁，它现在看起来死板，毫无生气。

We will take our break now, he said.

I stepped outside, for a moment, into the night air.

It was a cold night. The town was on a beach,

near where the wood had been.

I felt I had no future at all.

I had tried and I had failed.

I had mistaken my failures for triumphs.

The phrase *smoke and mirrors* entered my head.

And suddenly my teacher was standing beside me,

smoking a cigarette. He had been smoking for many years,

his skin was full of wrinkles.

You were right, he said, the way

instinctively you stepped aside.

Not many do that, you'll notice.

The work will come, he said. The lines

will emerge from the brush. He paused here

to gaze calmly at the sea in which, now,

all the planets were reflected. The driftwood

is just a show, he said; it entertains the children.

他说，我们休息一下。

我走到外面，在夜晚的空气中待了一会儿。

夜晚寒浸浸的。小镇在海边，

木头就来自这附近。

我觉得自己完全没有未来。

我努力过，但我失败了。

我总把失败错当胜利。

烟与镜这个组合语闪过我脑海。

突然，老师站到我身边，

抽着香烟。他抽烟多年，

皮肤布满皱纹。

他说，你那样做是对的，遇人

就本能地让到一边。

你会发现，这样做的人不多。

他说，作品会有的。画笔

会生出线条。说到这里，他停下，

平静地注视大海，此刻，

海水反射出所有的行星。浮木

只是一场表演，他说；是让孩子们开心的。

Still, he said, it is rather beautiful, I think,

like those misshapen trees the Chinese grow.

Pun-sai, they're called. And he handed me

the piece of driftwood that had broken off.

Start small, he said. And patted my shoulder.

4.

Try to think, said the teacher,

of an image from your childhood.

Spoon, said one boy. Ah, said the teacher,

this is not an image. It is,

said the boy. See, I hold it in my hand

and on the convex side a room appears

but distorted, the middle taking longer to see

than the two ends. Yes, said the teacher, that is so.

But in the larger sense, it is not so: if you move your hand

even an inch, it is not so. You weren't there, said the boy.

You don't know how we set the table.

That is true, said the teacher. I know nothing

不过，他说，我认为它挺漂亮，

就像中国人栽种的那些外形嶙峋的树。

那叫盆栽。然后他

把那块掉下来的浮木递给我。

从小处做起，他说。他拍了拍我的肩。

4

老师说，试着想一个

来自你童年的图像。

勺子，一个男孩说。嗯，老师说，

这不是图像。男孩说，

是。你看，我把它握在手里，

它的凸面就呈现出一个扭曲的

房间，但中段比两端要多花一点时间

才能看清。是的，老师说，确实如此。

但在更广泛的意义上，情况并非这样：你的手动一下，

哪怕移动一寸，情况就不一样了。你又不在场，男孩说。

你不知道我们怎么布置桌子。

说得没错，老师说。你的童年，

of your childhood. But if you add your mother

to the distorted furniture, you will have an image.

Will it be good, said the boy, a strong image?

Very strong, said the teacher.

Very strong and full of foreboding.

我一无所知。但如果你把你妈妈

加到扭曲的家具旁边，就会得到一个图像。

那图像好吗，男孩问，会留下强烈印象吗？

很强烈，老师说。

非常强烈，而且充满不祥之兆。

A SENTENCE

Everything has ended, I said.

What makes you say so, my sister asked.

Because, I said, if it has not ended, it will end soon

which comes to the same thing. And if that is the case,

there is no point in beginning

so much as a sentence.

But it is not the same, my sister said, this ending soon.

There is a question left.

It is a foolish question, I answered.

一句话

一切都已结束，我说。

什么让你说出这话，妹妹问。

因为，我说，如果还没结束，那也快了，

结果还是一样。而如果是那样，

连开始说这句话

都没有必要。

但二者不一样，妹妹说，很快结束不同于已经结束。

还剩下一个问题。

一个愚蠢的问题，我回答道。

A CHILDREN'S STORY

Tired of rural life, the king and queen

return to the city, all the little princesses

rattling in the back of the car, singing the song of being:

I am, you are, he, she, it is—

But there will be

no conjugation in the car, oh no.

Who can speak of the future? Nobody knows anything about the

    future,

even the planets do not know.

But the princesses will have to live in it.

What a sad day the day has become.

Outside the car, the cows and pastures are drifting away;

they look calm, but calm is not the truth.

Despair is the truth. This is what

儿童故事

国王和王后厌倦了乡村生活，

回城里去，小公主们全都跟着，

在车后座喋喋不休，齐唱系动词"是"的变位歌：

我是 am，你是 are，is 用于他她它——

但是车里

不会有变位，不会。

谁能说说未来？没人对未来有一星半点的了解，

甚至行星也不了解。

但公主们免不了要活到未来。

想到这些，这一天就变得多么悲伤。

车外，牛群与草场渐行渐远；

它们看起来很平静，但平静绝非真相。

绝望才是真相。这一点，

母亲和父亲心知肚明。所有的希望都已烟消云散。

mother and father know. All hope is lost.

We must return to where it was lost

if we want to find it again.

我们必须回到那希望消散处，

才可能再次找到它。

A MEMORY

A sickness came over me

whose origins were never determined

though it became more and more difficult

to sustain the pretense of normalcy,

of good health or joy in existence—

Gradually I wanted only to be with those like myself;

I sought them out as best I could

which was no easy matter

since they were all disguised or in hiding.

But eventually I did find some companions

and in that period I would sometimes walk

with one or another by the side of the river,

speaking again with a frankness I had nearly forgotten—

And yet, more often we were silent, preferring

the river over anything we could say—

一段记忆

一场病悄然降临，

病因从未确定，

尽管越来越难以维持

一切正常、身体健康

或生活愉快的表象 ——

渐渐地，我只想和与我类似的人在一起；

我竭尽所能找到他们，

而这绝非易事，

因为他们都有伪装或者躲了起来。

但最终我总算找到了几个同伴，

那段时间，我有时会

与这个那个在河边散步，

说话时又有了我几乎遗忘了的坦率 ——

然而更多时候，我们沉默无语，更喜欢

河流，而不是我们可能说到的任何东西 ——

On either bank, the tall marsh grass blew

calmly, continuously, in the autumn wind.

And it seemed to me I remembered this place

from my childhood, though

there was no river in my childhood,

only houses and lawns. So perhaps

I was going back to that time

before my childhood, to oblivion, maybe

it was that river I remembered.

河两岸，高高的泽地禾草

被秋风吹拂，静静地，毫无间断。

我似乎从童年起

就记得这个地方，虽然

小时候这里没有河，

只有房屋和草坪。所以，也许

我正慢慢回到童年之前

那段时间，回到遗忘之中，也许

我记得的就是那条河。

AFTERNOONS AND EARLY EVENINGS

The beautiful golden days when you were soon to be dying
but could still enter into random conversations with strangers,
random but also deliberate, so impressions of the world
were still forming and changing you,
and the city was at its most radiant, uncrowded in summer
though by then everything was happening more slowly—
boutiques, restaurants, a little wine shop with a striped awning,
once a cat was sleeping in the doorway;
it was cool there, in the shadows, and I thought
I would like to sleep like that again, to have in my mind
not one thought. And later we would eat polpo and saganaki,
the waiter cutting leaves of oregano into a saucer of oil—
What was it, six o'clock? So when we left it was still light
and everything could be seen for what it was,
and then you got in the car—

下午和傍晚

那些美好的黄金岁月，那时你即将死去，

但仍能和陌生人随意交谈，

随意但又很刻意，因此世界的印象

仍在塑造并改变你，

而在夏天，这座城市熠熠生辉，毫不拥挤，

尽管这时一切都变得更缓慢 ——

时装店、餐馆、搭了条纹遮阳篷的小酒馆，

有只猫一度睡在门廊里；

那儿凉爽，阴影憧憧，我想

我也愿意再那样睡在那儿，脑子里

一个念头也不存留。过后，我们会去吃烤章鱼和小锅奶酪，

服务生把牛至叶切碎放到油碟里 ——

那是几点，六点？所以我们离开时天还亮着，

一切都可以看出它本来的样子，

然后你上了车 ——

Where did you go next, after those days,

where although you could not speak you were not lost?

你接下来去了哪儿，在那些日子之后，

去了哪个你不会说话但不会迷失的地方？

SONG

Leo Cruz makes the most beautiful white bowls;

I think I must get some to you

but how is the question

in these times

He is teaching me

the names of the desert grasses;

I have a book

since to see the grasses is impossible

Leo thinks the things man makes

are more beautiful

than what exists in nature

and I say no.

歌

列奥·克鲁兹会制作最漂亮的白碗；

我想我必须送一些给你，

但在这些日子里

怎么送才是问题

他在教我

认沙漠草的名字；

我有一本关于它们的书，

因为不可能去看草的实物；

列奥认为人造的东西

比自然界中存在的

更美

而我不同意。

And Leo says

wait and see.

We make plans

to walk the trails together.

When, I ask him,

when? Never again:

that is what we do not say.

He is teaching me

to live in imagination:

a cold wind

blows as I cross the desert;

I can see his house in the distance;

smoke is coming from the chimney

That is the kiln, I think;

only Leo makes porcelain in the desert

可列奥说：

等着瞧。

我们制订计划

一起去徒步。

什么时候，我问他，

什么时候？不再有下一次了：

但我们不会说这话。

他在教我

怎么活在想象中：

一阵冷风

在我穿越沙漠时吹过；

我可以看见他远处的房子；

烟囱里冒出烟来，

我想，就是那座窑；

只有列奥在沙漠中烧瓷；

Ah, he says, you are dreaming again

And I say then I'm glad I dream
the fire is still alive

啊，他说，你又在做梦了，

而我说很高兴，我梦见，
火还在欢跳。

译者注

[1] 这里的原文是"空杯子",指的是《道德经》中的"器",中文原文是"埏埴以为器,当其无,有器之用"。

[2] 欧内斯特·贝克尔(Ernest Becker, 1924—1974),美国文化人类学家,他出版于 1973 年的《拒斥死亡》获得普利策奖,该书认为个体性格之形成本质上是拒斥死亡的过程,而世界上的大部分恶也正是拒斥死亡的需要所导致的。

[3] 原文是四个汉字的拼音"huli songli",但诗人自己说不记得是什么字,根据下一行英文的意思音译为"送礼护理"。

[4] 休利特和伍德米尔都是纽约长岛的小村庄。

[5] 往背后撒盐即驱邪。

[6] 小恩斯特,奥地利心理学家西格蒙德·弗洛伊德的外孙。失/得(Fort/Da)是弗洛伊德《超越快乐原则》中记录的儿童游戏,他观察外孙扔掉玩具又拉回,以此解释人与痛苦的关系。

致谢

《美国学者》（*The American Scholar*）

《自由》（*Liberties*）

《纽约客》（*The New Yorker*）

《纽约书评》（*The New York Review of Books*）

《巴黎评论》（*The Paris Review*）

《三便士评论》（*The Threepenny Review*）

一如既往地感谢莉萨·哈利迪（Lisa Halliday）。

文景

Horizon

社 科 新 知　文 艺 新 潮

上海文化发展基金会资助项目

合作农场的冬日食谱：中英双语版

[美] 露易丝·格丽克　著

范静哗　译

出 品 人：姚映然
责任编辑：李　琬
营销编辑：杨　朗
封扉设计：周伟伟
美术编辑：安克晨

出　　品：北京世纪文景文化传播有限责任公司
　　　　　（北京朝阳区东土城路8号林达大厦A座4A　100013）
出版发行：上海人民出版社
印　　刷：山东临沂新华印刷物流集团有限责任公司
制　　版：北京金舵手世纪图文设计有限公司

开本：850mm×1168mm　1/32
印张：3.75　字数：52,000　插页：2
2024年3月第1版　2024年3月第1次印刷
定价：49.00元
ISBN：978-7-208-18732-0/I·2134

图书在版编目（CIP）数据

合作农场的冬日食谱：中英双语版／（美）露易丝
·格丽克 (Louise Glück) 著；范静哗译 . -- 上海：
上海人民出版社，2024
书名原文：Winter Recipes from the Collective
ISBN 978-7-208-18732-0

Ⅰ.①合… Ⅱ.①露… ②范… Ⅲ.①诗集－美国－
现代－汉、英 Ⅳ.①I712.25

中国国家版本馆CIP数据核字（2024）第029839号

本书如有印装错误，请致电本社更换　010-52187586